The Paci Pixie

Magic
Meadows

written by Amy Perreault & Cheryl Hajjar

illustrated by Steven Perreault

Publishers Cataloging-in-Publication Data

Perreault, Amy.
   The Paci Pixie / written by Amy Perreault & Cheryl Hajjar ; illustrated
by Steven Perreault.
   p.cm.
   Summary: Follows the night flight of the Paci Pixie as she helps a
small child give up her pacifier and then takes it to the woods to be made
new for a new baby.
   ISBN-13: 978-0-615-47150-1
   [1. Pacifiers (Infant care) - Juvenile fiction. 2. Pixies - Juvenile fiction.
3. Stories in rhyme.] I. Title. II. Hajjar, Cheryl. III. Perreault, Steven, ill.
                                        2008943322

Copyright © 2009 Indigo Magic, LLC
Printed and bound in the United States of America

Indigo Magic
Publishing

   45 Jackson Street
   Methuen, MA 01844

To order additional copies please go to www.indigopixies.co

This book is dedicated to Nicholas, Maiya & Dylan,
because we love them more than they love their Pacies

Once upon a midnight hour,

The Paci Pixie saw a flower.

She blessed it with her pixie wand

To take its gift before the dawn.

The crystal blossom was the flower.

Its golden nectar gave her power.

The flower wished the Pixie well
And watched her cast her magic spell.

She spread her wings into the night

And flew off on her mystic flight.

She perched upon the windowsill,

As through the glass the child lay still.

She waved her wand and in she flew.
'Twas time to make the paci new.

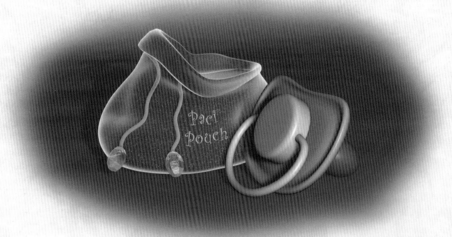

She touched her wand to the child's head,

Spilled pixie powder, then she said,

"I fly to thee, oh little one.

You must be brave—the time has come.

Your paci you won't need again.

I've made you strong, my precious friend."

With the flash of her wand,

in the blink of an eye,

The Pixie soared the starlit sky,

And all the forest came alive

When the Paci Pixie then arrived.

The forest friends had work to do—
Time to make the paci new.
They worked their magic through the night;
By morning they were out of sight.

USED
PACIES

Deep in the forest near a stream,
The Paci Pixie now could dream.
She rested her wings in the warm sunlight.
Soon she'd take another flight.

And in the morning a child awoke,
Remembering the words the pixie spoke:

"Little Pixie, I do believe
In the magic that you conceive.
I'll run and tell every boy and girl
That you help us grow in a grown-up world."

from:
Paci Pixie

The End